Wanting more

As a child, I never thought life would be so hard. It was all fun and play, no worries, no stress, just being a kid. Growing up in the projects in which back then who knew what projects were. All I ever wondered was" why were there so many bricks". Didn't have money to travel through the city to see anything different, didn't know any better. Enjoyed going outside playing little sally walker, or Kool-Aid, and going in to what I called my winter wonderland, my room. As a child, the younger of 2 and the only girl, I had everything I wanted, talking dolls, doll houses, games everything fit for a princess. I never understood the sad looks on my friend's faces, weren't they happy too, what was wrong, didn't they have the things I had.

I quickly found out that the answer was, no.
Even though we stayed in the projects my mom
always had a job she paid full rent and bills, but
hey wait,didnt everybody do that. I got to realize
that again the answer was, no. Everybody didn't
work, pay rent or bills. All my friends didn't have
the luxuries that I did, but when you are young
you don't understand why.

As I got older growing up in the project wasn't so
easy and happy times weren't so happy. My
friends, were not my friends, they were actually
people who didn't like me because they envied
what I had, Huh,really,envy me, but why, I stay
in the projects too, I wasn't that lucky. My
highlights and rewards were going to the malls.
The malls were like heaven when I was younger,
I knew that we would go to the mall and get to
eat out and maybe just maybe get something
new.

Getting older meant venturing out. I was always the smartest in my class so I went to gifted schools that were far away from the projects. In my traveling to school I started to see that, there weren't any more brick houses that stuck together, what were these things that were separate and beautiful, that when I saw another world and that was neighborhoods with houses. Oh how I wished I could stay in one. I was always known as a project girl, and although that's where I had the most fun I didn't want to be there anymore.

Being smart may seem to be a good thing but those same people that envied what I had, also envied what I was, and that was another strike added to my name. So I stayed away from my neighbors and became friends with other people like me, the smart ones. As the years went by I got older and my interest started to sway away from the books and into something new, the boys. I always knew that god made boys, but why was I starting to feel different towards them, instead of wanting to punch them, I wanted to say I love them, and that is where life changed, things got hard, and there was no turning back.

Start of life

Wow, I made it out the projects, here I am standing in a house, a real house who would have thought my family would have come this far. But how would I fit in, would anybody like me, well I'm going to find out. By now I'm in high school and its o.k. I have a lot of friends and there are lots of boys, boys, boys. I had one special friend that hung out with and that was Nikki. Nikki was fun, she was very outgoing and we were the best of friends. Nikki at age 16 had her own car and was my personal driving instructor, and with two 16 year olds and a car means trouble. Everyday Nikki and I hung out just walking around and really doing much of nothing. Nikki was known in school to be a real bitch, mainly because she was popular with the boys, it has been said that she gave blowjobs to anybody that gave her money, and although Nikki would never admit it, I'm not sure that the rumors are really rumor. Nikki and I really connected; she had also come from a poor neighborhood and had been sheltered all her life like me. But unlike me, Nikki was fearless and didn't have any cares in the world. She lived her life as if there was no tomorrow and didn't care about what people said or thought about her, and like I said Nikki had been labeled as a hoe. I always saw her with different boys coming from the locker room or with an older student in their cars. Nikki was my friend and regardless of what people though I loved her like my sister. She always stood up for me and she got me out of my quiet shell. Although we were like night and day we were also like one, and we were having the times of our lives as teenagers but who knew the good times would be cut short.

It was a Friday night and we were bored. I had stayed at her house because my mom worked late.

"Nikki, we have watched this stupid movie 3 times, let's go outside...or better yet let's take the car". I saw Nikki's eyes light up when I mentioned taking the car, and on top of that her mom wasn't home either so now was the perfect opportunity.

"Do you have money for gas Kayla, and where are we going anyway, we are 16 and too young to get into anywhere". Said Nikki.

"Well we can go to Keith's house, I talked to him earlier and you know he stays with his grandmother and older brother and he gets to do anything he wants, so we can hang out there".

Now Keith was my little boyfriend that I had who I had met on the bus. He was tall, dark and handsome, and he was 18 and in his last year in school. Keith went to a private school and always had everything he wanted. He inherited money from his father's passing due to a hospital mistake, and his mother went crazy soon after and was put in a mental hospital. He always treated me like a queen, but since I wasn't allowed to date, I had to sneak and see him. Keith was much more experienced than me; he had lost his virginity at the age of 15. He never pressured me into sex but I knew he craved it and as much as I wanted to please him, I wanted to make sure the time was right even though he said he loved me, I wanted to be sure. I believed that he was being faithful even though he was filled with temptation every day from females in the school. I saw how they would look at him when we were together, they knew I was younger and also knew that we hadn't had sex. We did other things that made him happy because I wanted him to preview what he had in store for him.

We got the car, got gas and arrived at Keith's house. He met us at the door, with his brother and immediately came out and said that his friend was having a house party and he wanted us to go. We agreed to go, we parked Nikki's mom's car and got into his brothers. We were so excited about going to a party, but when we got there no one seemed to be our age and there were mostly guys and only a couple girls. Nikki who was the outgoing one fit right in , and went right to partying and dancing with a group of guys. I followed her just to advise her not to drink and to stay within site so I could keep track of her. I then went and sat down with Keith. Keith was a good guy, he never got into any trouble and had dreams of going to the military after graduating said that he wanted to marry me when I was 18 and pay my way through college. We sat and talked and danced and had a good time, and I kind of forgot about Nikki. I told Keith that we better go find her and leave because her mom would be getting off work in a while, but Keith told me that he would go find her and for me to wait. Nikki's mom was a nurse and she worked often at night so Nikki snuck out a lot. Keith was taking so long that I decided to go look for her myself, and on my way there I found Keith's brother Kevin and he said he would help me look. We looked all around for her and there was no sign of her. We found Keith and he said that someone told him that they thought they saw her go upstairs, but he hadn't checked there yet. So we went up the stairs and there were a lot of people making out and drinking, but we didn't see her. There was one door that was closed and I knocked, no one answered so I opened it and on the floor laid Nikki trembling and crying. Her clothes were ripped and hair was messed up.

"Nikki what happened to you?" Yelled Keith.

As for me I just stood there I didn't know what to do or to say.

"Kayla dial 911 and get the police here, I think she was attacked and she is hurt, Nikki you got to tell us what happened."

"I,I,I went to the bathroom and when I came out there were three guys in this room and they told me to come in and have a drink. I told them that I couldn't drink and that I had to go, but they kept insisting and said it was only a little. So I came in and took the drink. One of the guys shut the door and said that I had a nice body and he wouldn't want it to go to waste. I told him I was only 16, but they were all drunk and I was too, next thing I know I woke up and my clothes were ripped and there was guys standing everywhere around me, they were laughing and pointing, I looked down and I was bleeding, Kayla I was raped and I don't even know if it was by one guy or multiple guys because I can't remember what happened,. I remember the room spinning and I felt numb and I couldn't do anything but lay there. When I woke up one of the guys said I deserved it for being fast. Kayla we got to get out of here I have to get home". Cried Nikki.

By this time the guy that stayed in the house came up and said he didn't want any trouble and that we had to get out. We tried to explain what happened and he just kept saying get out. So we left, the police hadn't come and Keith drove us to the car. He had to drive us to Nikki's house because she wasn't in the right state of mind to drive and I didn't have a license. So he drove us to the house as his brother followed him. As we got out the car the brother told us that it was best not to say anything because we would only cause trouble with ourselves. I didn't understand that but just agreed to keep quiet. I took Nikki in the house and told her she better get cleaned up because her mom would be home soon. She proceeded to clean herself as she cried and cried and cried. About 30 minutes later her mom came home, she looked in on us to make sure we were alright and then went to her room and immediately went to sleep. Nikki made me promise that we would never talk about what happened and that everything would be o.k, but as the weeks went on everything wasn't o.k. About 6 weeks had passed and things were o.k. at first.

What's done in

the dark

We never talked about the incident, but I could see the pain in Nikki's eyes and she seemed to be distant. Nikki was not the same, she wasn't being herself, that spark and spunk that I loved about her was gone. She seemed nervous and she was really quiet. There had been no more sneaking out, heck no going out the house period for us. Things kind of got a little boring. I wanted to help her, talk to her, but I didn't know what to say. So for the most part we just sat in silence. One day in school after lunch. It was after lunch period and Nikki came up to me and said that she need to leave and wanted me to come with her. I had never cut school but it seemed to be important so I agreed. As we left school I asked where we were going. Nikki went to explain how she had been sick and throwing up and her period hadn't come. Now although Nikki was outgoing I didn't know of a boyfriend that she had so I didn't even have the thought of pregnancy. We went to the clinic and after checking in the first thing she had to do was pee in the cup, I waited for maybe an hour and then Nikki came out from the room with tears in her eyes, walking tight past me. I jumped up and followed her.

"Nikki wait up, whets wrong, what did the doctor say?"
"The doctor said that I was pregnant Kayla, what am I going to do, how am I going to tell my mom? Nikki not only had pain in her face but fear as well.
"Nikki how can you be pregnant, Oh my god that night at the party. Nikki we have to tell your mom" It was like I was talking to myself because Nikki just stared into space as we waited on the bus. She asked me to ask my mom if I could

come over because she wanted me there when she talked to her mom. My mom said it was o.k. and didn't question me why. My mom worked to jobs, and my brothers were away in college so she didn't want me staying alone a lot.

As we arrived at Nikki's house my heart started beating fast as though I was the one with the problem. Nicki's mom was sleep so we waited. After about 2 hours she came down and asked us did we want something to eat. As she went to hug Nikki she saw that something was wrong.

"Nikki, baby you o.k. what wrong, you sick. Say something, Kayla what wrong what happened." questioned Nikki's mom.

"I think that Nikki better tell you"

"Mom, I messed up, I'....Imp sorry I didn't mean for it to happen. I went to the doctor and they said I'm pregnant, mom I'm......"

Before Nikki could say another word, her mom

slapped her so hard she fell to the ground.

"You tramp, you whore, and I work all damn night and you around here laying around"

"Ms. Ward it's not her fault she didn't do this"

"Well who did it to her?"

"Kayla stay out of it, mom I messed up I slept with an older guy I met, I didn't even really know his name." Why was Nikki lying to her mom, and making herself look bad. Why didn't she tell her about that night? Nikki's mom asked me to leave and said that she didn't know if I would be seeing Kayla for a long time. As I walked out the door I felt as though it would be the last time I would see my best friend.

I went home and gave my mom the biggest hug, I told my mom what really happened, she was mad about the fact that we snuck out and took a car but was glad that it didn't happen to me. She explained that it's better for me to stay out of it and let Nikki deal with it herself, so I did. I didn't see Nikki anymore in school and she didn't return any of my phone calls. I had heard through the grapevine that her mom had moved the family away. Nikki was gone and there was nothing that I could do.

What happened with Nikki kind of had me depressed, so depressed that I began to take her place with the boys in school. Nikki was my only friend and now she was gone and Keith had already graduated. So I decided to have sex with some of the boys, give blow jobs and other things just to get some attention. I got involved with the wrong crowd. I started smoking weed, taking pills and drinking just to make myself feel better. What was I doing to myself; I knew I was better than this I was becoming what everyone said I would be coming out the projects. Things had to change, so I went to my mom for help.

Got into rehab and got back into school. I started

writing Keith and his words were very

encouraging, he said that he would come back

for me one day. Life here I come.

Growing Up

It was almost time for graduation, I still hadn't heard from Nikki, Keith had gone to the army and was stationed in Texas and my brother was in Europe doing art. We still kept in touch and talked almost every day so things were good, but I still missed my friend and thought that I would be graduating with her. Graduation ceremony was beautiful I graduated top of my class, and who would have thought a little girl from the projects making it to the top. Keith had surprised me and showed up to see me walk across the stage. After the ceremony came another surprise. He proposed to me, I was in shock and I said yeas. Keith Had kept his promise and came back to me. My mom was very supportive as I told her I would finish school and she gave me her blessings. Well the surprises didn't stop there. Keith told me that before we went any further he wanted me to know that he had this other life in Texas and that he was involved with a woman there but she had passed away from cancer and she had a daughter, I asked him what did that have to do with anything. He said that the woman didn't have any family and he helped her take care of her daughter and when she passed she left him to be in charge of her. He said the little girl, Nakesha was almost two and that he had dropped her off at his mom's and wanted me to meet her.

"So you are saying you have a daughter Keith, I don't think I'm ready to be a mom to someone. How could you not tell me, I know you were dating other people so was I but to be so serious with someone that she leaves you her child, how could you not tell me"

"Kayla it was hard leaving you and yes I knew that you would see other guys and I really wanted to wait for you and didn't mean to get involved with her, well her name was Cameryn, but she was different she helped me through times when I was missing my family. When I met Cameryn her she was just getting out of a divorce, she was 5 years older than me and her daughter was a baby. She had explained to me that her and her husband had been trying to conceive but had trouble, so they adopted Nakesha but soon after her husband left her. so I felt inclined to help her and that's how it started" Keith went on to tell me that the little girl and him were very close and when cameryn found out that she was dying he felt more inclined to take on the role of daddy so he married her and adopted the baby. I cried as he told me the story, and although hurt by the fact that he kept this secret, it made me love him more because he was a stand-up guy, and how could I turn him down and say no. I couldn't I told him that I would give it a try and do my best to make it work. Keith was stationed back in Cleveland and had told me that after his 4 years was up he was not going to sign back up for the military. And here we were and instant family, it was hard for my mom at first because she was scared that it would ruin my life and that I wouldn't have time for school. But I did it I went on to finish school with a degree in nursing,

Keith had left the military and got a job at a major company for he as well had got his degree while in the army. We got married and the ceremony was beautiful. We kept it small. It was everything I could ask for. The only thing missing was my best friend Nikki. I always pictured we would be by each other's side when we got married, but I stood alone.

Reunited

We had officially adopted Nakesha who was going on 6 and had accepted me as her mom for she was really young when her real mom passed. It was winter and I was in the store shopping for boots when I heard someone call my name.

"Kayla is that you" said a females voice.

"Oh my god Nikki, oh Nikki I thought I would never see you again how have you been, where have you been"

"Well I been well, I can't complain. After the whole pregnancy incident my mom moved us to Texas,"

"And the baby"

"I gave the baby away, I didn't even know what the baby was, and I didn't want to know." Said Nikki.

Nikki went on to talk about her time in Texas and how difficult it was to be young and pregnant in a strange town, in where she felt alone. She said her mother kept her home schooled and didn't allow her out of the house. She was sick all the time from the pregnancy and was depressed because of it. Nikki wanted to keep the baby but her mother wouldn't allow it. She downgraded Nikki to the point where Nikki said she started to believe that she couldn't be a good mom. Although Nikki didn't want to know the gender of the baby, she eventually found out along with information about the adoptive parents.

"But enough of me, whose little girl is this?"Nikki said with a puzzled look

"This is Nakesha, Keith's daughter, Keith and I got married"

"Well she looks too big to be your daughter how old is she"

"She is almost 6, and well it's a long story." I

asked Nikki to come to my house and we could

talk. She did and I explained the situation with

Keith and then she told me what had been going

in her life. She said that after the baby she went

and got her GED and got a job working at a

restaurant. She said the baby drove a wedge

between her and her mother and that after

finding work she moved out and moved in with

some guy she worked with. She said that they

were engaged and that he was very supportive

of her and wanted her to go to school and better

her life. She said that they had decided to move

back to Ohio and find work. I told her that I

would help her anyway I can, and hoped that we

could reconcile our friendship and be close.

Nikki seemed to be alright but there still was this

pain, what was it that she wasn't telling me. I'm

just glad that she is back in my life.

Nikki found a place close to where Keith and I

stayed, about a mile away. I helped her get a part time secretary job at the hospital where I worked. It was kind of hard because I worked long hours and so did Keith and Nakesha was left in daycare all day and all night, something had to give. I sat down with Keith for a talk.

"Honey we need to make some changes, I don't think we are giving our daughter the attention she needs, I mean the both of us see her maybe 2 hours a day. We can at least only leave her in daycare a couple hours after school and maybe my mom can help."

"Your mom?, ha I doubt it she never liked the idea of me & you" , how about Nikki she stays up the street and only works in the morning I'm sure she can use the extra money" said Keith.

"Nikki would be perfect, let me ask her. That way Nakesha doesn't have to do daycare at all Nikki can pick her up from school."

I approached Nikki at work with the idea and she though it was perfect. She said she could use the extra money because she and her husband Rick were trying to conceive. I asked her was she ready to do that , although it had been years since she gave her baby away, I didn't think she was mentally ready.

Nikki started right away picking up Nakesha. They instantly bonded which was surprising because Nakesha doesn't really like too many females. She actually was really good with her as far as being a mother figure for her, but there still was that hidden pain that you could just feel when Nikki was around her.

"Keith can you believe that they are laying nurses off at the hospital, is the recession gone that bad that they need to take way the people that saves lives"?

"Yeah I know but it will be o.k. if you are on the chopping block, that way you can be home with Keke and we can work on a baby of our own". Said Keith.

So I did get the news that I would be one of the nurses getting laid off. So home here I come. I had to let Nikki know that I wouldn't need her to take care of Keke anymore, and she let me know the she also got laid off. She was fine with it and it gave us both more time to rekindle our friendship.

A year had passed and it must have been a good mating season because we both got pregnant Nikki was 9 months and I was 8, and we both were huge. We spent our time shopping for baby clothes, decorating baby rooms and eating at the malls as our time was getting closer to delivering our babies. It was a bad blizzard outside and we were on our way to pick up some items for a duel baby shower. "Nikki I don't know I think we better turn around its really slippery out here and I just have a bad feeling and I"

"Kayla calm down we will be o.k. If we don't get the rest of the things for the party now we will be running around at the last minute and we both know we can't run" Nikki laughed.

The next thing I remember is the car going out of control and then waking up in the hospital.

"Keith, where I am what happened?".

"K, you and Nikki were in a bad car accident". Said Keith.

"Oh my god my baby where's my baby, Keith where's my baby" I screamed.

"K, calm down they did a C-section and by the grace of god, he is o.k., it was a boy he weighed 6 pounds 13 ounces.". Said Keith.

I cried" I want to see him, where is he?"

"He is being checked and luckily you only had a
mild concussion"

"But wait a minute, what about Nikki"

"Nikki will be o.k. she has a broken leg, but K the
baby didn't make it. They were not able to save
her baby."

"It's my fault. I should have listened to my gut
feeling and went home. I have to see her Keith,
take me to her or I will go myself"

Keith wheeled me to her room. When I got there
her back was turned. I called her name and she
didn't respond. We went to the other side of her
bed and I poured my heart out to her and her
husband explaining to them how sorry I was and
how I wish I could take away their pain. Rick
gave me a hug and said it wasn't my fault. But
Nikki she was different, and the look on her face
said hatred. I tried to hug her when all of a

sudden she screamed,

"Get off of me, I hate you, I hate you Kayla. You have everything and I have nothing. You and Keith have a child, why did god take mine and leave yours, I hate you all don't ever come around me again" cried Nikki.

I was stunned, I couldn't say anything, I just asked Keith to take me back to the room. I sobbed all the way back. Hours later the nurse brought the baby back in the room and although I was overjoyed with happiness of my baby, I felt guilty and feared that I have lost my best friend all over again.

The pain I felt for her almost overcame my happiness with my own baby. I didn't know how to comfort or help Nikki. I felt guilty about being happy, when I knew my friend was dying inside. I have to get my emotions together and try to live my life.

Mending

Fences

It's been so hard having Nikki so close to me but so far away from my heart. She still wasn't talking to me. I called and called till my fingers got tired. So I stop calling, and decided to move on with life. My stress was putting a strain on my marriage the baby who we named Keith Jr was 2 years old and Nakesha was 10, I was only working part time and Keith was struggling trying to make ends meet. He had been working long hours and would come home so tired we wouldn't see each other or talk. I decided that things had to change and soon. Nikki still stayed by me, her husband left her because she never got over the loss of the baby and she kind of flipped out, and from what I heard she was using drugs. But she still maintained her job at the hospital and kept up a good front.

Keith's birthday was coming up and I wanted to do something special for him. "Keith baby, are you staying off from work for your birthday

today?"

"I will if you want me to, I know we haven't spent

the time together like we should be, I miss you"

"Well we can take the kids to my mom, who

surprisingly offered to baby-sit, but I'm not

complaining".

"Well we can go to the cabins, and go from

there"

I actually felt like my life was coming together.

But every time my happiness came, the devil

was right around the corner. Me and Keith went

to the cabins and had the best time and things

were starting to look up. Then here it comes the

time when the happiness disappears. Another

four years passed and everything was perfect

the kids were getting big and doing great. Keith

and I had never been better. I had a new circle

of friends, a new job and a new look on life. And

although Nikki moved but before she did we sort of made up. She writes me every now and then to ask about the kids but other than that I don't see her. I hope she is o.k. and doing well.

"Kayla I have something to tell you, promise not to get upset" said Keith in a disturbing voice.

"Baby what is it?"

"I got a call today, it was from my ex-wife's sister, and she said that the adoption agency contacted her because Nakesha's birth mom was looking for her. I mean, why would she look for her now, Keke is almost 14, she doesn't know she is adopted, this would break her heart. Regardless her aunt gave the adoption agency my information to contact me, so they could ask me if it was o.k. to talk to the birth mom"

"Keith, I can't believe this, we have been the only parents she has known why would she want to interrupt her life now, it doesn't make sense"

"Well I guess Keke has the right to know but I just don't think now is a good time, but maybe I can talk to the agency and get the birth moms name and do a little investigating to see what kind of person she is, but right now I will just keep this between us, here is the number I can call them in the morning"

"O.k."

Even though I said o.k. I don't know if I really meant it, and I figured that Keith would be busy so I took it upon myself to find out what was going on. I called the agency and explained to the agency that we didn't think it was a good time for Keke to know about it and maybe when she was older we would tell her. The agency rep said she wasn't aware of anyone making any calls but she would send me the information on the birth mom and that was the end of that, at least I thought. Over the next couple of weeks I couldn't do anything but think about how Keke would feel when she got older and found out that her mom was looking for her and we prevented it. Would she hate us, would she want to be with her birth mom? I am her mom, I have been there for her and I won't stop now, I love that girl and even though she knows I am not her real mom, I am all she has had in the last 8 years and she never knew that Keith wasn't her real dad, and that's the way it was going to stay.

"Mom somebody's at the door" yelled Keke.

I opened the door and too my surprise, "Oh my god, Nikki is that you, uhh uhh you look great, come in"

"Oh Kayla I know I haven't been a good friend and I just want to make it up to you, I am back in town and feeling great. As you may have heard I did go through a rough patch and was on drugs and under great depression. That is one of the main reasons I left, I went to rehab and got myself together. I got remarried and later after we get settled I will let you meet my husband. Oh these kids are just getting so big" said Nikki. "Speaking of, since you have this new man are you thinking of having more kids?"

Nikki looked at me in the strangest way and said" Kayla, we tried but doctor says I won't be having any more kids. I had a lot of damage done when we had the accident and I lost my baby. Kevin, which by the way is my husband's name, he thought about adoption or even having a sergeant mom. And that got me thinking about my baby I gave up and where she may be in at this point in her life. Just think her and Keke could have been best friends like us, they were the same age. Sometimes I regret giving her away but I know it was for the best. I am at the best place I can be in my life and I feel that I could be a great mom to her now"Nikki said sadly.

We talked and laughed for hours and her husband came by later after Keith got home and we all had a good time. Days had passed and I still hadn't received the information from the adoption agency, so I called and the lady said that she mailed it the same day, so I asked Keith had he seen any mail from them, and he said that he was shocked that I didn't mention to him that I had call, and I told him that he hadn't told me if he called or not either, but nerveless he said he hadn't seen any mail from them.

I and Nikki was back on track, we were both back at the hospital and happy with our marriages and life. One day when we were having lunch she expressed to me that she had tried previously to find the daughter she had given up but had no luck, because the adoptive parents didn't want her to contact her. What a coincidence because I told her that Keke's mom had been trying to contact and find her also, but when I took it upon myself to contact them again regarding her name and other information, the adoption agency rep told me she had changed her mind. Well I wasn't going to press the issue, but I did feel bad for Nikki, she wanted kids so bad and she was so good around mine, I wish I could help her.

Things are not

what they seem

Life still was good, and things were moving along. I had taken some days off because Keke was sick. I took her to the doctor and they couldn't pin point the problem, they wanted her to stay overnight to run some additional test. I contacted Keith and we both agreed on it, but we were confused why, for she only had symptoms of a cold. We all stayed at the hospital including little Keith. The next day the doctors said they had the results, and ask could he speak to us alone. He told us that Keke has leukemia and that it was in a progressed stage. But they could treat it with transfusions and chemo. I was confused, Leukemia, how could she have leukemia, the doctor continued to tell us that her blood type was rare and that it may be hard to find someone that matched hers, he explained that everyone should be tested, friends, family, anyone we could think of. For a while me and Keith were in shock and couldn't figure out why god would let this happen to our little girl. But we had to be strong for her. I don't think Keke really realized the severity of the disease and for now that was a good thing. She thought it was cool to be in the hospital and have food delivered to us and through all the pain we felt for her, she smiled. A lot of us got tested, except for Keith, he was so busy at work, and I would think that he would take the time out for his daughter to get tested but his explanation is he worked so much to keep his mind off of Keke but that he would go soon. In the meantime I tried to contact the adoption agency, I figured I wouldn't tell Keith, because he would freak out, but I thought maybe it was time to find both parents, and that maybe one of them was a match and they could help. The rep I had spoken to a while ago had retired but the new rep that had the file was happy to give me so information. All she had was a last telephone number and address of the birth mom and no information on the birth father. I figured I better start digging now the sooner I can find something about them the better it will be for Keke whether Keith liked it or not. I figured I would get Nikki to help me since she stayed in Texas a long time ago, maybe she still remembered street names and neighborhoods, although I wasn't so sure how she felt about doing it since she had given up her child too. But it doesn't hurt to try.

"Nikki, I want to ask you something, but feel free to say no because I know it may be difficult for you. Well you know Keke needs a donor and none of us were a match, I decided to look for her birth mom and all the agency was able to give me was an address and not a name, do you think maybe I can tell you the info and you may

knew where in Texas it is?"

"Sure Kayla, I would do anything for Keke, what

is the address?"

"14678 township rd., and there was a number

213-879-7654, anything ring a bell?"

Before I knew it Nikki ran out of the house

crying, I guess it really was too much for her and

that the mention of Texas hit a nerve. I figured I

wouldn't bother her again about it and decided

to take a trip to Texas. I just told my husband

that I was going on a business trip and that I

would only be gone 2 days, I told him that I was

going to Chicago so he wouldn't be suspicious. I

had never lied to my husband before, but this

was for a good cause. Since they were keeping

Keke in the hospital Keith took off to stay with

her and little Keith stayed with my mom. I still

hadn't heard from Nikki, but I didn't have time to

worry about her. I took a flight out to Texas and when I got to my hotel I got the help off a concierge. She gave me directions to the address and got me a taxi. When I got to the house I was a little nervous, because if the birth mom was still staying there, this would be one hell of a blow. I mean what would I say, Hi my name is Kayla and I think I have your daughter that you gave up and she is sick can we have some of your blood, ha well maybe I won't say these exact words. I knocked on the door and to my surprise when the woman came to the door she was an older lady, and I was in so much shock that I couldn't say anything.

"May I help you?" said the lady.

"Oh I, I think I have the wrong address I'm sorry". I ran so fast back to the taxi and told him to pull off immediately. What in the world is going on, at this point I felt like I was in a bad dream. I checked right out of the hotel and caught the next flight right back home. There was no need for me to stay in Texas any longer. When I got home I went to see Keke, and she wasn't doing good, the doctor said that she needed that blood transfusion soon or things wouldn't be good. I went to the house and Keith was there. He was surprised to see me and asked what happened. I just couldn't tell him at that moment so I told him that the meeting was canceled and they sent us back home. He looked terrible, as though he had been crying all day. He told me that when I left he gave blood and wasn't a match. For days I sat in disbelief in what I saw in Texas, I called Nikki, she finally answered and I asked her to come over. When she got there I couldn't say anything to her at first, she stared at me and I stared back. I broke the ice and asked was there something that she needed to tell me.

"I, I know that ad-address that you had for Keke's birth mom. That was my address when I lived in Texas, my mom still stays there, Kayla what is going on ,why would my address be attached to Keke's birth mom" cried Nikki

"I know that was your address, I went to Texas, when I got to that home, your mom answered the door. I figured she wouldn't recognize me after all these years so I was in so much shock that I just told her I had the wrong house and I left. Nikki what was the name of the adoption agency that you went through and did they give you any information regarding the adoptive parents?"

"The name of the agency was Happy Homes, and they couldn't give me the name of the adoptive parents because it was a closed adoption. My mom later gave me some names in which I thought were the names of the adoptive parents, only later to find out she was just lying to throw me off.

"OHHH MY GOD, Nikki that's the same adoption agency, could Keke be your daughter"

"I don't know, no she couldn't be. This is crazy Kayla"

"Well the only way to find out is through a DNA test, Nikki oh my god we have to get to the hospital, if you are her mom, you could help her let's go while Keith is at work, and I don't want him getting upset."

We went to the hospital and they got blood from Nikki and first tested it for a match for Keke, but it wasn't. They said they would put a rush on the DNA test, that we would have it in 24 hours. I couldn't think. What have a done, what if Keke is Nikki's, what if Nikki wants to take her, and for what her blood didn't even match. What have I done, Keith is going to kill me. Nikki and I went in the room to see Keke, she was sleeping, and Nikki stared at her in tears. I left out the room to talk to the doctor. He informed me that it was very critical to get a donor in the next five days. I told him that we were running out of options, and then he asked what about my husband.

"Huh, what about him. He said he came in got tested and wasn't a match"

"No I don't have him on record coming in" the doctor said as he walked away.

What was going on, why would Keith lie, I was sure going to find out. When I got to the house Keith had left me a note saying he was on his way to the hospital. So I went and picked up my own child from my moms, I need to spend some time with him and figure out what was going on. The next day the lab called and said they had the results, I asked if they could just tell me over the phone, and Nikki's DNA matched Keke's, oh my god Nikki was her mom. I immediately called Nikki and for a while there was nothing but silence, then Nikki cried, and I cried and she said that she would wait till Keke was healthy to even think about anything.

I got myself together and went to the hospital, when I got there Keith was still there asleep. I gave him a hard nudge to wake him up and asked if I could speak with him in the hall.

"Keith what the hell is going on, why would you lie about getting tested for Keke, what is up with you" I screamed.

"I just, I didn't have time and plus I'm scared of needles, baby I'm sorry"

"You're sorry, yeah you are, and you can get your sorry ass down to the lab and give your blood, come on I'll gladly walk you down"

Keith looked at me in the strangest way, we

went to the lab and I made sure that he gave blood. Meanwhile I didn't tell him about Nikki, and decided to go home and think.

My cell phone rang and on the other line was a lady that said she was the adoption agency and said she was just checking to see how Nakesha was, because Keith had called and told her not to bother us because she was sick and that if she found out she was adopted it may make the situation worst.

"Excuse me, I asked. "You say my husband called"

"Yes he called not too long before you did because I was surprised you still wanted the address, he said that you guys were not interested in finding the birth mom"

"Well Keke isn't doing well but thanks for calling".

What is happening, why is Keith going behind

my back, well before I could gather my thoughts the lab had called and said that Keith was the rare match. Who would think that someone who is not related would be a match, even the doctor said it would most likely be a family member.

Well I didn't have time to analyze the situation. I rushed back to the hospital to tell Keith, but the doctor had already informed him and was in the process of doing the transfer.

It would be days before we would know if the transfer worked and there were still things down the road that could happen to her. I was so stressed out, and had all these questions going through my head that I decided to go out and get me a drink. I got a friend of mine and we went to a bar called the L Spot. It was for the grown and sexy and although I didn't feel sexy, I was definitely grown. I was sitting at the bar when I was approached by a man who said I looked familiar, ha, the classic line"dont I know you" but the more I looked at him he did look familiar, as a matter of fact he was the guy that stayed in the house where Nikki was raped, his name was Malcolm. We began to talk and he asked what ever happened to Nikki, I told him the whole breakdown of her life and how she got pregnant from the rape and gave the baby up. He went on to say that he was sorry and always wished he could help but didn't want any trouble, he went on to say he knew who done it.

"You mean to tell me that you knew who raped her and was scared to say something"

"I wasn't scared I just didn't want to get in any trouble because you guys were under age anyways, including the guy that did it. What was his name ken or no it was Keith, the guy that you guys came with"

"What, what did you say" at this point I felt anger

coming on.

"Keith, you don't remember the little guy that you were with, Kevin's little brother, have you heard anything about him?"

"Hmm, yeah, I married him" I said angrily as I walked out the bar. I cried all the way home, as I dropped my friend off. I couldn't think. I drove around for hours, my phone rand constantly, Keith was calling. How could this be, Keith, a rapist, what does this mean. Did he rape my friend, father her baby, and marry the adoptive mom, does he even know.

I decided to go to Nikki house and talk to her. When I got to the door, she opened it and asked what was wrong. She immediately said not to worry about the situation about her being Keke mom. But I sat her and her husband down. She had already told him that she was Keke mom. I told the both of them what I learned at the bar.

Her husband jumped up and said that he was going to kill Keith, Nikki just sat there in disbelief and then she said,

"You know what, that night, I thought I saw Keith in the room but things in my mind were so distorted that I couldn't remember, Oh my god Kayla, Keith raped me"

"I know Nikki. I'm sorry, it must have happened when he claimed to have looked for you and was gone so long. C'mon we have to go"

We made a stop and then went to the hospital. I went to Keke room and she was sleep but Keith wasn't there. I saw him in the cafeteria, he went to hug me and I went with my first reaction, I slapped him as hard as I could the walked away. Nikki was standing behind me, she cried out "how could you". Before Keith could say anything the police arrested him. As he was being taken away he looked at us and I think he put two and two together, and he just dropped his head. So you can figure now that we stopped at the police station, although Nikki's case was years old, it was still valid. We gave the police the information we found out and had Malcolm come down and give his statement. The next day I went to the police station to visit Keith. He couldn't even look at me.

"Keith how could you, all this years, and it was you, and you knew she was my best friend, and then you marry me. And what's worst is, did you know that Keke was your daughter?"

"Yes I did, when I got to Texas I found out that Nikki was there and by me being in the military, I had some strings pulled and found out who adopted the baby. I befriended Cameryn and got close to her, I never told her my relationship to her child. I felt bad for what I had done to Nikki and felt I had to take Keke and raise her. But

Kayla I loved you and still do. I was young, drunk and stupid. I wanted to tell you so many times but knew that you would leave me and I couldn't take that's-But how did you find out"

"I have also contacted the agency and they gave me an address for the birth mom, and I went to Texas the day I told you I had a meeting, and when I got to the house Nikki's mom came to the door, I left without saying anything, I told Nikki what happened and we put it all together. Nikki took a DNA test and that's when I found out that she was her mom. I didn't figure out your part until the night I went out to the bar and ran into Malcolm, he remembered me after all these years. He told me that he had known you raped Nikki but didn't say anything. Keith How could you?"

"Kayla, I'm sorry, I'm so sorry, I wish I could take it back"

"Well you can't, and as far as me and you we are over, I talked to Nikki and we are going to keep things the way they are, as far as you, you can go to hell, Nikki is pressing charges and for now we will just tell Keke that you did something bad and are going to jail, we will wait till she is older to explain. I hope you rot in hell, don't call us Keith, this is goodbye"

"Kayla please, please, please just take care of my baby, I love you, and I'm sorry"

I walked out. Nikki did press charges and they charged him with rape and sentenced to only 5 years but it was some justice. Me, Nikki and her husband decided to out of state and find homes close to each other. All I could think about is what Keith would do when he got out, but right now I had to go on with life and pick up the pieces and start over.

The recovery

Well Me, Nikki and Rick got the kids and moved to Detroit. I didn't want to be too far from my mom. We both moved in to the city in the same area actually right next door to one another in some townhouses. Nakesha was doing a lot better. Her doctors in Cleveland recommended some in Detroit so she could get the best care. She was starting to ask why her dad went to jail. She was naive. She was very smart for her age. So with Nikki's help I decided to explain to her the whole situation. I started with how much her dad and I loved her then went back, back when Nikki was raped. I didn't make it sound bad, I just said they were drunk and had sex. Nikki told her that she was too young and decided to give her up. We explained about her adoptive mom, and how her dad met her but told Keke that her dad didn't know that she was his real daughter. We made her dad look descent, then we said he went to jail because Nikki was too young for him to have sex with and that when it came up later that they were the real parents, the cops took him to jail. She kind of understood but still was a little confused. I know she adored her dad and I didn't want him to look to be a villain in her eyes. She was excited about having two moms, but had no desire to stay with Nikki. She also decided to call her aunt Nikki, which in Nikki's eyes that was just fine.

A couple years had passed and Keke was going on 16. We were planning on throwing her a sweet 16 party. She had made a lot of friends from school, and we decided to let some of her friends from Ohio come as well. My mom told me that Keith would send letters for us, but I told my mom that I didn't want her to forward him, to just trash them. I knew my mom would keep them anyway. A couple days before Keke birthday I check the mail, and there was a letter forwarded form my mom, and it was from Keith. I stared at it for hours then decided to open it.

Dear Kayla,

I am not sure if you have read any of my letters, for you have never written me back and I do understand why. How is Keke, she has to be getting big by now. I think about you guys all the time. Speaking of her 16th birthday is coming up. Wow she is almost a woman. Well I will be going up for early release for good behavior hopefully I get out and could try to mend things with you and the rest of the family. Please let Keke know I love her and tell little Keith that his daddy will always love him. I wish you would write me back, send me some pictures or something. How is your life, have you found someone new, if so I hope you are happy. When I got the divorce papers I didn't want to sign them, but I know that I was wrong and that your life had to go on. Well I hope that I can mend things with us when I get out, until then I love you guys.

P.S- Tell Nikki I am sorry and I hope she forgives me one day.

Keith

Damn him, who does he think he is. Forgive him after what he has done. I can't think about it right now. I had to plan for Keke party and besides my brother who I haven't seen in 8 years was coming back home, and I was excited. My Brother Dion had been in Iraq for the last 4 years, and before that stationed in Europe. Although he wrote and we always talk and exchange pictures, he didn't have any desire to come back to the states, and I don't blame him. He always sent us money, and paid all my mom's bills, for he had his own art gallery and other businesses and was doing well for himself. Dion was married, and then married again, and he had 2 kids. I'm excited to see him and he is thinking of moving his family and our mom to Detroit.

His New wife's name was Camie and she was the mother of his 3 year old daughter. Camie was beautiful inside and out, she was a good mom and good wife. Even though I had never met her, we always talked on the phone and wrote letters to each other. But like I had seen in Nikki before, Camie had this pain in her face, as if she was missing something.

"Camie, Dion, oh my god how nice to see you" I said as I hugged them tightly.

"Well what about me" said my mom, for she had come too.

"Mom, I see you a lot, but come here give me a

hug, love you"

"Kayla, I have been waiting to see you for years, nice to finally see my sister in law, we got some catching up to do" Smiled Camie.

We all caught up, cried, laughed, talked more, ate, and even had some drinks, for at least 8 hours. Everyone was tired and decided to go to bed. Everyone except for me and Cameryn.

"So Camie, how are you, is everything o.k.? I just get this feeling that something bothers you"

"Kayla, I am over joyed and also taking in a lot of emotions from being back in the states. Before Europe I stayed in the states and a lot went on, and none of it good, but enough about me. I am so excited that we all are going to be living in the same state. How is everything for you since Keith? Have you talked to him, does he call, is your friend involved in Keke's life? Oh forgive me, I'm babbling."

"Well yes Keith calls, I don't talk to him but I do allow him to talk to Keke. I heard he will be getting out soon for good behavior. Just hope he doesn't head this way. He found out where we were and got my number through one of his contacts, but if he knows what's best he will stay away."

"Wow, just bring back memories, I once was married before and had a husband , Kenny was his name, well at least that's what I thought, I had a baby too, but-t-t, I , I can't talk about it now, just forget it." Cried Camie as she ran out the room.

Whatever was bothering her was not good. She has been through a lot of pain and was not going to pressure her about what had gone on. But she said she had a baby, had as if in a past tense manner, where is this child now, well anyway off to bed for me.

"Mom I want to take drivers Ed in school, and I need my birth certificate, do you have one for me?" asked Keke.

"Umm, no I don't but I can call the state of Texas and request and pay for one"

I instead just went online and requested one, then thought about it. Nikki must have one. I called Nikki and she told me that her parents thought it be best if the adoptive parents put their name on it. So I had the adoptive moms name but not the dad. So of course I had to contact the jail and get the information from Keith. He called me and told me that he actually had the birth certificate changed when he married Cameryn, and had his name on it, when he finished he thought that he would try and have conversation with me but I hung up. Those days were gone, and I had moved on and actually was dating a guy I met named Mike, who was very good to me so far. Well about 3 days after I submitted the form online, someone called me from the state of Texas. They told me the only way I could get the information is if I had accurate information on both parents, and that the father's name was incorrect. Huh, what was going on, Keith said his name was on there. Well I had to figure out what to do next. I guess I had to do a little research on Cameryn's marriage, but had no time to think about it at the moment because Nikki and Rick were celebrating their anniversary.

Nikki invited my brother and his wife to come. Which was perfect, they had got a house two blocks over and really didn't know a lot of people in the city, and this way they could mingle and meet some neighbors.

"Cammie this is my best friend, Nikki Reynolds, oops I mean Nikki Dawson now". Camie paused and walked away.

"I'm sorry Nikki forgive my wife, she hasn't been feeling well and still trying to get adjusted" said Dion

"Hmm that was strange, well anyway Nikki congratulations on you and Rick, and here's to many more" I say as I toasted the couple. I couldn't get out of my head how weird Camie had acted towards Nikki and was determined to see what was wrong.

"Hey Camie, is it o.k. if I come by?"

"Sure come on over"

I arrived at my brother's house and Camie was still in her robe at 2 p.m.

"Kayla, has Nikki always stayed in Detroit?"

"No she used to stay in Cleveland with me, why do you ask?"

"Oh no reason her name just sounded familiar. As I said before I lived in the states and was married, actually twice. My first husband was killed, and my second husband, well he was someone I should have researched before marrying him. He was younger but he charmed the pants off of me." said Camie as she stared into space.

"Wow, so you said you had a baby, what happened to the child?"

"My baby, I loved that baby, I loved her as if she was my own, I'm sorry Kayla I can't do this" Cried Camie.

I left because I wasn't going to push her to talk if she didn't want to, but she said she loved the baby like it was her own, what did that mean, was the baby her husbands and did she adopt. Well I decided to ask my brother and he said that she rarely talks to him about the situation and that all she told him was she no longer had a child. So I decided to leave it alone, I had to concentrate on my own family. Since I didn't get anywhere with the birth certificate I decided to research Cameryn Little, which was Keke's adoptive mom full name. Under the marriage certificates she had a Nathan Jones, and a Kenny Williams listed as her husband's name. But what was weird was I didn't see Keith's name. I mean I know he said he married her when he found out she was dying so why isn't in the system. Just as I was going to sit and write Keith someone was knocking at my door, it was Camie.

"Hey Camie I didn't know you were coming by what's up?"

"Hey Kay, are you alone?"

"Yeah come in"

"I'm sorry for just dropping by like this but I felt

that I should explain the night of your friend's anniversary. See when I stayed in the states I stayed in Texas and like I said I was married, twice. My first husband and I wanted a baby so bad but he couldn't have kids and so we decided to adopt. We adopted a newborn baby girl in a closed adoption. I never saw the mother and I learned her named by accident. Her name was Nicole Reynolds and she was around 16, 17. After adopting the baby who I named Destiny, she was so precious and my husband and I were so happy. Not too long after he was killed, and I was left to raise her by myself, I was lonely, and depressed and that when I met my 2nd husband Kenny. Kenny was like my savior, he kept me company and helped with the baby, but I didn't know a lot about him. He said he had no family and hat his mom and dad had passed and he was an only child. He said he worked for

FBI and couldn't discuss his job so I didn't ask and he also said that we had to move to Europe for an assignment he had, we married after only 2 months, we had settled in Europe and . I had gone back to work after a while and Kenny had said he would take a couple weeks off to watch destiny, until we found daycare. It worked out for 2 days and then on that 3rd day I came home early because I had been calling him at home and he wasn't answering, I called his cell phone and it was disconnected. When I got home I saw no sign of him or the baby. I waited for hours and then I called the police, of course they said since he was my husband just to wait a little while longer. Well the next day came and they put out an amber alert, and I waited, waited and waited for my baby and then nothing it was like they never existed. I gave them his name and they said that they couldn't find any information on him and that the FBI didn't have anybody employed with that name. Next thing I know years had passed. I had been even more depressed and had a nervous breakdown, I had no way of really getting back to the states and was staying in like a shelter and working part time there, and that's where I met your brother he and some of the other military people were helping us feed the homeless. Dion talked to me daily, got me a job, and I was alive again, but never forgot my baby and when I heard Nikki's name it freaked me out"

"Who wait a minute are you saying that you adopted Nikki's baby?

"Yes-s-s, well I think it's the same name and if she stayed in Texas it's here, Destiny would have been almost 17 now, just think she could have been Keke best cousin"

"Umm so is Camie your name?"

"No its Cameryn"

"Look this is a lot for me to take in Camie, I ,I guess we should tell Nikki But ,look just give me a little time,o.k, and I'll talk to you later" I said as I suggested she leave.

This is major. What the hell is going on? Am I dreaming? If her husband's name was Kenny then where does Keith fit in because he never mentioned Europe and that would mean he lied to her about his name and kidnapped Keke? I didn't know what to do, I couldn't bring myself to tell Camie who Keke was, and I guess my mom never mentioned the fact that Keke was really Nikki's daughter to my brother. So I called my mom and gave her a small breakdown and told her to keep quiet. Next thing to do was call Nikki, so I did and I explained the whole story. She was in disbelief and agreed with me that we shouldn't tell Camie about Keke because although she wasn't the birth mom, Keke apparently was kidnapped, but how did Keith get her. Keke was almost 17 and looking at colleges, this could ruin her life and I couldn't stand for that. I had to pull myself together for my family, I still have a young son to take care of, and this was too much.

More Secrets

For months I would make up excuses as to why Keke couldn't come over my brother's house, I didn't want them asking her questions. I had gotten a call from Keith, decided to talk to him. He said he was getting out in 2 weeks and wanted to see his kids. I didn't mention Camie or what she told me. I just told him that he could come here and meet us at the mall or something if he had a way to Detroit but he couldn't come to my house. So since I had a father's name I decided to order her birth certificate and get her driving lessons. The two weeks had passed and I hadn't heard from Keith, oh well it didn't matter to me. I heard the phone ring when I answered it. On the other line was Camie.

"Kayla, Kayla I need you to come to the house."

"Camie what's wrong?"

"I thought I saw my ex-husband, I thought I saw Kenny at the store asking for directions, I ran out and came home right away"

"You say you thought you saw Kenny, in Detroit why would he be here"

"I don't know, maybe I'm just seeing things, ever since I talked to you about it, I've been having flashbacks maybe I'm just paranoid" cried Camie as she shook back and forth crying.

"Camie would you happen to have a picture of Kenny, I mean just in case we need to look out for him"

"Yes I do. I kept a picture of him, why I don't know. Hold on let me get it"

She got the picture and it seemed as though my eyes were moving in slow motion, I looked at the picture and it was Keith, and her holding the baby. I told her that I would take it and make copies. Oh god what was I going to do. I immediately went to Nikki and showed her. She couldn't believe it. Who was this man I had loved and married? He was a liar, a kidnapper, a rapist. My first thought was to run and take the family to another state but I couldn't do that to them again, little Keith was finally adjusting and I had met a wonderful man. I feel in my heart that I should tell Camie but if she wanted to try and take Keke that would tear my heart apart. I decided to take a trip to Ohio and visit Keith's brother, for I thought maybe he would go there. I took Nikki with me and left Keke with my mom, I had to get some answers from Keith.

"Kayla, oh my god how are you, how my niece and nephew. What are you doing here? And Nikki how are you" said Kevin

"I'm looking for your brother is he here?"

'No, he called me when he got out asked to wire him some money and last I heard he said he wanted to surprise the kids in Detroit"

"WHAT, when was this?"

"A day ago, I would assume he's there by now. I do know he has your mom's address. I advised him not to go there but you know how he is when it comes to his kids. And Kayla, he has changed. He is into got, he got saved and he just wants to start over as a dad. He understands you have your own life but he told me he just wants to help you support the kids"

"Thanks Kevin, I have to go" I said as I ran back to the car.

I got in the car and called my mom, she wasn't picking up and just as I was leaving a message, Camie picked up the phone.

"Hey Kay, I'm out of breath running to the phone"

"Camie what are you doing there, where is my mom?"

"Oh she went to visit one of the church members in the hospital and I'm here with the kids, I hope you don't mind, is everything o.k., where are you?'

"Umm, yeah I'm o.k. just tell my mom to call me when she gets back, are the kids there?"

"Yeah they are in the front yard playing"

"Oh can you tell them to come in. I don't want them out"

"Kay, girl it's nice out and their hanging with their friends. I'm watching them and besides Keke an old lady now" laughed Camie

"CAMIE JUST TELL THEM TO COME IN NOW" I screamed.

"Kay I will, what's going on?"

"Nothing I just, nothing I will be home in about 4 hours. I and Nikki are on our way home, I will see you soon, and sorry for yelling, I just have a headache"

"No problem, be careful"

The only thing that was going on in my mind was

that I hoped Keith was nowhere close to my mom's house, If Camie saw him it would be bad. I remember Camie saying that if she ever saw him again she would kill him. It seemed like it was taking forever to get back to Detroit, we were maybe thirty minutes away when I got a call from my mom.

"Kayla, you need to come home now"

"Mom what's wrong?"

"Keith is here and Camie is ranting on about him stealing her baby"

"Mom I'm almost there"

When I got there everyone was in the house, Mom, Keith, Keke, Keith Jr, and Camie. I walked in and Camie was fussing at Keith and I heard him saying he was sorry.

"Keith what are you doing here?" I asked

"Baby I just wanted to see my kids"

'KEITH, his name isn't Keith its Kenny. Kay this

is my ex-husband, you have to call the police"

"Camie calm down, and just listen"

My mom took the kids in the bedroom. I approached Camie and she was shaking and crying.

"Camie sit down"

"I don't want to sit. Kenny must have followed me here, KENNY WHAT ARE YOU DOING HERE WHERE IS MY CHILD AND WHAY ARE YOU SAYING YOU WANT TO SEE YOUR KIDS" yelled Camie.

"Camyrn I"

"Keith just shut up and let me try to explain it to her"

"Why do you keep calling him Keith, his name is Kenny, Kenny I'm going to ask you one more time what you are doing here" Camie said as she stood up and grabbed her purse

"Camryn I'm sorry, everything I did was for a

reason" cried Keith

Just as he was going to explain, Keke ran out, I tried to get her to go back into the room, but she refused.

"Kenny, go to hell" cried Camie as I heard a loud noise.

"Daddy Noooooooooooooooooooooooooooo" screamed Keke as she ran in front of him.

The next couple seconds seemed to be unreal because I didn't know what was happening. It felt as though time stopped.

"Keke ,Keke "cried Nikki as she ran over to her. I couldn't move I was stuck, I saw Keke on top of Keith, but then I saw Keith move. Camie had tried to shoot Keith and the bullet hit Keke.

"Keke baby" I said as I ran over by her and Nikki.

"D-D-Daddy, did she say daddy?" said Camie with a strange look on her face.

"Camie what have you done, what have you don't to my baby" cried Nikki, as called 911 and tried to stop the bleeding. Keke was shaking and bleeding, the bullet had hit her in her chest. The next thing I saw was Keith run over to Camie trying to strangle her. By this time my brother was coming in the house.

"Keith get off my wife" said Dion as he pushed Keith down.

"Keith, oh my god Kay is this your husband, and why are you saying Keke is your baby Nikki"

"Because she is, Keke is my biological daughter and you adoptive daughter, and you just shot her" cried Nikki. The ambulance was coming but Keke wasn't breathing and by the time they got there they tried to revive her and she was gone, just like that.

"Oh my god, Kay did you know about this, why didn't you tell me" said Camie

"I didn't tell you because this was my family Camie, mine, Keke was my daughter I raised her, and yeah I found out about Nikki being her mom, that's why Keith went to jail, he raped Nikki when she was younger, he is Keke's real father, and I guess he found out about you changed his name and took her from you, And look what you have done, you killed her, you killed her, you killed her" I cried.

My brother was trying to make since of everything for he had been left out of the loop. The police arrived and we gave statements, and they took Camie down to the station. My brother went with her. My first reaction was to attack Keith, this was all his fault, and he was responsible for this whole mess. I didn't have the energy to yell, all we all could do is cry. I asked Keith to talk to his son and to never step foot at my house or my mom's house ever again.

The Aftermath

It took a while for the family to recover. The loss of Keke hit everyone hard. My brother had moved back to Europe with the kids, he said he couldn't take it here anymore. Camie was charged with murder and was in jail. I married Mike and Nikki and Rick were still together. Little Keith suffered a lot in school so I pulled him out and decided to home school him. Keith Never came back. He had transferred one hundred thousand dollars to me for his son. He had gotten the money from an inherence form his uncle. He said that he would never bother us again until little Keith was old enough to want to see him. The nerve of him, how dare he ruin my life like that? Keith still had some things that I kept stored away in the attic. I wanted to rid them as fast as I could. It was mainly just papers, pictures and mail. As I was throwing away the things I came across what seem to be

a letter from a woman named Ann, I opened it
and read it:

"

"Dear Keith,

I told you that I would never contact or
think about you, but my conscience is getting the
best of me. You see even though I turned my life
over to god, my past came to biter me in the
butt. Back then I though what we did was the
right thing to do, and for me I needed the money
at the time. I recently got married and tried to
see, and I myself got into a bad accident and
now am unable to have kids. I try to tell myself
that you loved your wife and what you did was
all for her, but what about her friend. It was
wrong of us and I will never tell our secret to
nobody else but I pray that one day god stops

punishing me for my sin My life has been nothing but shambles since, I never worked as a nurse after that. Switching those babies was wrong, letting your wife believe her child lived and her friends child dies was not right and its eating me up inside because I can't talk about it to no one but you other than that I will take it to my grave. I hope this letter finds you, and I hope you got the life and family you deserve. You won't hear from me again, take care.

Ann

"

Oh my god, what is she saying, I can't breathe,

is she saying Keith Jr isn't my child, O-O k I
have to calm down. I read the letter at least 50
times and every time I read it, the words became
clearer and clearer. I know I should say
something especially since Nikki was my friend
and it would be the right thing to do, but what
about me, I can't afford another loss and I won't.
Damn Keith for what he has done, but as he
lady in the letter said, this I will take to my grave.

Life went on slowly but surely. I still can't
believe all this happened and didn't know how
Keith could be this person that was so
mysterious. I often thought about Camie, and
kind of felt for her, for she was a woman scorned
and wanted to end the life of a man who took
hers. But instead ended Keke's life. Keke didn't
deserve this but I know that she is in a better
place, and is at peace. Nikki was thinking about

adopting which would be good for her because she needed someone else besides Rick to love. For me I was hoping that I could put this pain behind me. My life was never my own, and everything I thought I knew, I didn't. It was like I was in a bad dream, but I wasn't it was reality. All I could do is pray and move forward, because who said life was easy!

About the Author

Latoya Marie Jackson

Born and raised in Cleveland, Ohio in which she

still resides. First time Author, in hopes to

continue writing fictional and also children's

books in the future.

Made in the USA
Charleston, SC
23 February 2012